MW00974401

Behind *the* Scenes
at the Hospital

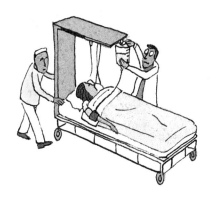

by **Marilyn Miller**
illustrated by **Ingo Fast**

RSVP
RAINTREE
STECK-VAUGHN
P U B L I S H E R S
The Steck-Vaughn Company

Austin, Texas

Copyright © 1996, Steck-Vaughn Company
All rights reserved. No part of this book may be reproduced or utilized in any form
or by any means, electronic or mechanical, including photocopying, recording, or
by any information storage and retrieval system, without permission in writing
from the Publisher. Inquiries should be addressed to: Copyright Permissions,
Steck-Vaughn Company, P.O. Box 26015, Austin, TX 78755

Published by Raintree Steck-Vaughn Publishers,
an imprint of Steck-Vaughn Company
Developed for Steck-Vaughn Company by
Visual Education Corporation, Princeton, New Jersey
Project Director: Paula McGuire
Production Supervision: Barbara A. Kopel
Electronic Preparation: Cynthia C. Feldner
Art Director: Maxson Crandall

Raintree Steck-Vaughn Publishers staff
Editor: Pamela Wells
Project Manager: Joyce Spicer

Library of Congress Cataloging-in-Publication Data
Miller, Marilyn F.
Behind the scenes at the hospital / Marilyn F. Miller: illustrated by Ingo Fast.
p.   cm. —
Includes bibliographical references and index.
Summary: Explains the functions of different areas of a hospital
such as the X-ray unit, the laboratory, the intensive care unit,
children's ward, and the maternity ward.
ISBN 0-8172-4087-X
1. Hospitals—Juvenile literature.   2. Hospital care—Juvenile literature.
[1. Hospitals.   2. Medical care.]   I. Fast, Ingo, ill.   II. Title.
RA963.5.M535   1996
362.1´1—dc20   95-8868   CIP   AC

Printed and bound in the United States
1 2 3 4 5 6 7 8 9 0   IP   99 98 97 96 95

Table of Contents

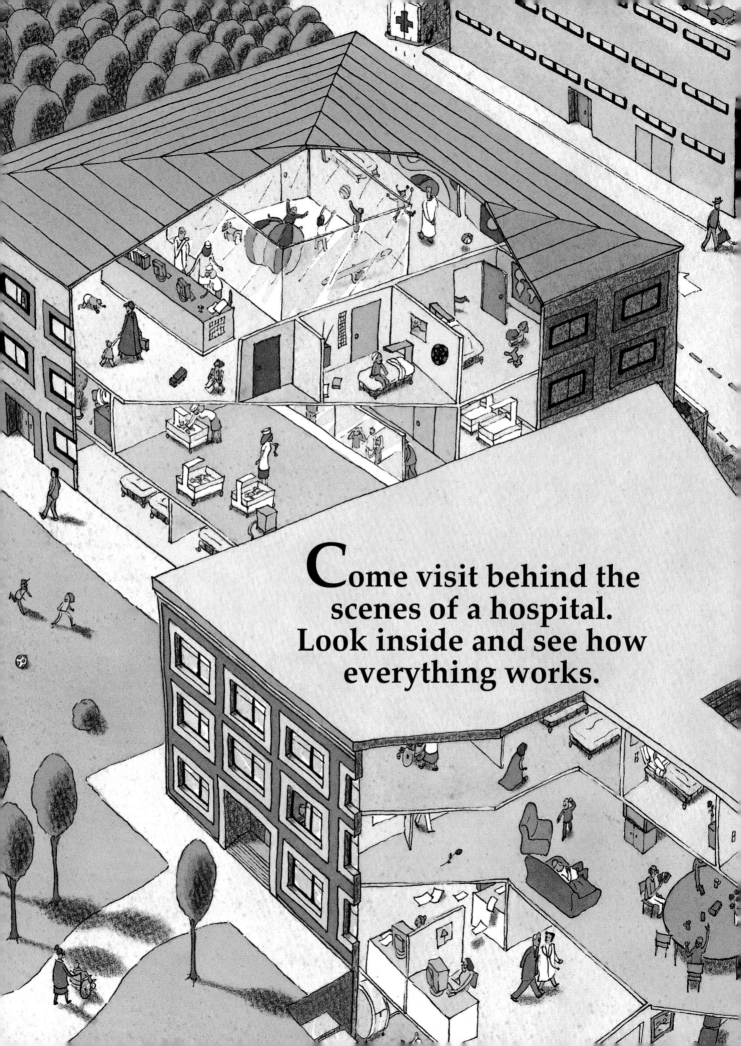

Come visit behind the scenes of a hospital. Look inside and see how everything works.

EMERGENCY

MEDICAL

5

Checking In

Patients check in to the hospital at the admissions office. An admissions worker asks them questions about their health. The worker also asks for any special medical information. These answers help doctors and nurses care for the patients.

At the admissions office patients also say how they will pay for their hospital stay. See the worker who is waiting to show the patient some papers. These are special forms to be filled out. The worker also assigns the patient to a room.

Do you see the nurse putting a plastic identification (ID) bracelet around the patient's wrist? It shows the patient's name and lots of useful information such as her blood type. The ID bracelet may also say that she is allergic to aspirin or needs a special diet.

Here comes a new patient. Notice the bag
with things for a hospital stay.
The bag contains a bathrobe,
a toothbrush, slippers,
a toy, and books
to read.

Taking Pictures

Patients have pictures taken of the inside of their bodies in the X-ray unit. The pictures show if something is wrong or if a bone is broken. Workers who use the machines are called technicians.

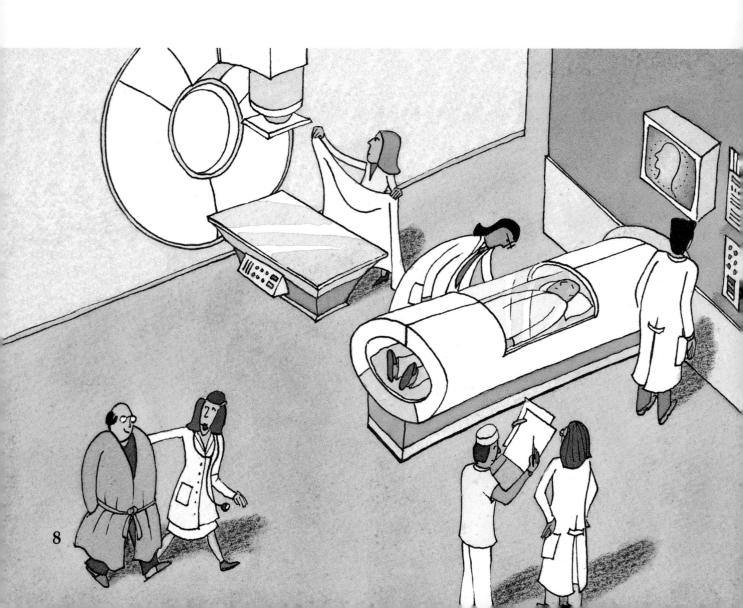

Do you see the doctors reading X-ray films? The films look like the negatives of pictures taken with a regular camera.

Two special machines produce computer-made pictures of the inside of a patient's body. One machine uses X-rays. The other machine uses radio waves and is shaped like a tube. Both machines take very clear pictures.

The patient in the tube is going to have pictures taken. Notice the screen above the machine. Doctors can read these pictures while they are being taken.

Here is a technician helping the patient put on an apron and a cap. These clothes protect the patient from unnecessary exposure to harmful rays.

9

Lab Work

One way doctors can tell what is wrong with a patient is by looking at a little of the patient's blood and urine. These tests are done in the lab. "Lab" is a short way of saying "laboratory."

Notice the trays of samples. The label on each sample tells which patient it came from.

Do you see the lab worker looking through the microscope? The microscope magnifies, or enlarges, things. The worker is checking a sample of a patient's blood.

Here is a nurse with a blood sample. Sometimes a sample is taken by pricking the patient's finger with a small needle.

Find the workers holding the tray of samples.

Operating Room

A team of doctors and nurses does surgery in the operating room (OR). The room must be sterile, or completely clean. That way, the patient will not become infected, or sick, from germs.

Everyone is wearing masks, gloves, and caps to protect the patient from germs. Even the walls, floors, and ceilings are washed down with strong cleanser.

Do you see the nurse helping the surgeon into his operating clothes? She also hands him the tools for surgery when he asks for them.

Notice the tray with tools and supplies. One tool is the surgeon's special knife called the scalpel.

Here comes a nurse carrying liquid medicine. Patients are often given this through tubes in their arms.

Special Care

Very sick patients receive special care in the intensive care unit (ICU). Notice that each patient can be seen by the nurses at all times.

Do you see the patient who is hooked up to several machines? One machine records the patient's heartbeat. Sometimes machines help people to breathe. The machines show on TV screens how each patient is doing. Nurses watch for sudden changes.

Here comes a new patient to the ICU. Notice the bottle hanging over the stretcher. It is already giving liquid medicine and food. This liquid will help the patient grow strong again. It flows into the patient's body through a tube in his or her arm.

Find the nurse carrying the medicine tray.

Stocks of Medicine

The medicine for patients is stored in the pharmacy. Pharmacists and their helpers work here. First, the doctors and nurses decide which drugs patients need. Then the pharmacists prepare the right drugs for each patient.

Do you see the pharmacist sitting at the counter? She is keeping a careful record of the drugs in the pharmacy. She does not give out any medicine unless a doctor orders it for a patient.

Here is the medicine carrier waiting for the elevator. He is delivering the medicine for the nurses to give to the patients.

Food for the Patients

Food workers prepare meals for patients in the kitchen. Do you see the workers taking food as it moves past and putting it on meal wagons, or carts?

Sometimes a patient must eat special foods because of his or her illness. Doctors write down the type of diet a patient must follow. A specially trained worker called the dietician makes sure patients have the food they need to grow well again.

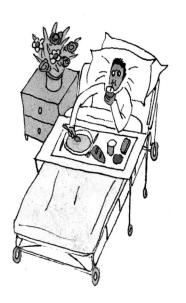

Here is a patient eating from his tray. The back of the bed is raised so that he can eat sitting up.

Keeping Clean

Dirty laundry from the hospital is taken to the laundry. Here, workers make sure that patients have clean sheets and towels. The laundry also cleans doctors' and nurses' uniforms and the special gowns that patients usually wear.

A large machine presses, folds, and stacks clean sheets. Do you see the worker removing the towel from the dryer? It will be folded and put on a wagon. Then towels can be brought to each room.

Here is a patient waiting while a worker puts clean sheets on her bed. Dirty laundry is collected from each hospital room every day.

Physical Therapy

Some patients are helped by specially trained workers in the physical therapy unit. Illness or injury can cause some part of the body not to work correctly anymore. Physical therapy helps patients to use the part again or make it stronger. Sometimes they are helped to use the part more easily.

Do you see the worker watching the patient lying on the large ball? The patient is exercising her back muscles.

Here comes a patient using a walker. The worker teaches the patient to strengthen her leg muscles until she can walk by herself again.

The Children's Ward

All children are in the children's ward. They eat their meals in bed like other patients.

They can play, read, paint, and draw in the playroom. Sometimes special visitors like circus clowns perform for them.

Do you see the nurse taking the baby for a ride in a stroller? The nurses are trained to work with children.

Here are parents saying good-bye to their son on his first day in the hospital. Sometimes a parent can stay overnight. The mother or father or a grandparent may sleep on a cot in the child's room.

Emergency!

People are treated in the emergency room (ER) when they are injured or suddenly become very sick. Sometimes an ambulance rushes a patient to the ER. Emergency medical technicians (EMTs) may give the person liquid medicine or oxygen. They also use an emergency method to start a person's heart and lungs working again.

ER is very busy. It never closes. The staff handles many different kinds of emergencies. Do you see the nurses at the desk? The computers there store medical information about patients.

Here is a doctor writing down a record of the patient's treatment. Most people who come to the ER can go home after they are treated. Some are moved to a hospital room. There they receive more treatment.

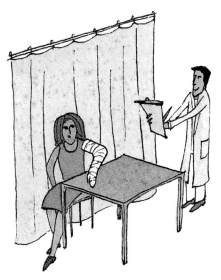

Find the boy with a bandage on his hand.

It's a Girl! It's a Boy!

Mothers and their new babies are cared for in the maternity ward. Most mothers and babies stay from twelve hours to two days. Nurses teach the new mothers and fathers how to diaper and feed their babies.

Do you see the mother holding her baby? She is about to feed him. Babies cry to let their mothers know when they are hungry. Sometimes the baby sleeps in a baby bed in the mother's room.

Here is a mother taking pictures. Visitors may go in the mother's room. They may not go into the nursery. That is a special room where babies stay when they are not with their mothers. Visitors can see the babies through the nursery window.

Glossary

The **admissions office** is where patients check in to the hospital.

The **children's ward** is a special ward where children stay together.

The **emergency room (ER)** is where people are treated when they are injured.

The **intensive care unit (ICU)** is where very sick patients receive special care.

The **kitchen** is where patients' meals are prepared.

The **lab** is where workers look at patients' blood and urine samples. They try to find out what is making the patients sick. "Lab" is a short way of saying "laboratory."

The **laundry** is where patients' sheets, towels, and special gowns are cleaned. The laundry also cleans doctors' and nurses' uniforms.

The **maternity ward** is where mothers and new babies are cared for.

The **operating room** is where a team of doctors and nurses do surgery on a patient.

The **pharmacy** is where medicine for patients is stored and given out.

The **physical therapy unit** is where patients are helped to use their bodies again. Patients may also be helped to make their bodies stronger.

The **x-ray unit** is where patients have pictures taken of the inside of their bodies. X-rays give doctors information about parts of the body that cannot be seen from the outside.

Further Readings

Bauer, Judith. *What It's Like to Be a Nurse.* Mahwah, New Jersey: Troll, 1990.

Bauer, Judith. *What It's Like to Be a Doctor.* Mahwah, New Jersey: Troll, 1990.

Butler, Daphne. *First Look in the Hospital.* Milwaukee, Wisconsin: Gareth Stevens, 1991.

Ciliotta, Claire, and Livingston, Carole. *Why Am I Going to the Hospital?* New York: Carol Publishing Group, 1992.

Howe, James. *The Hospital Book.* New York: William Morrow, 1994.

Index

J 362.11 MILLER
Miller, Marilyn F.
Behind the scenes at the
   hospital